All the Way Under

Written by Jyotsna Sreenivasan
Illustrated by Elizabeth Wolf

PEARSON

I didn't plan to tell a lie or to get into trouble. It just sort of happened. Katie, my cousin, had asked me to stay with her family for a week during the summer. Katie and I were both nine. We were going into fourth grade in the fall. We both enjoyed riding bikes, playing games, and dancing to our favorite music. For the first few days, we had a wonderful time. But that all changed when Uncle Jack decided that he would take us to the beach on his day off.

I tried to act happy about going to the beach. It was my first time. I should have been excited. But I didn't want Katie to know I hadn't learned to swim yet.

"You can swim, can't you?" Uncle Jack asked as he turned into the beach parking lot the next day.

"Uh-huh," I nodded. It wasn't really a lie. I had started taking swimming lessons three times, but I never finished. The real problem was that I was afraid to go all the way under. Just thinking about putting my head in the water made me very nervous.

As soon as Uncle Jack parked the car, Katie jumped out of the back seat. She was ready to go swimming. Uncle Jack and Aunt Lisa grabbed the beach towels and umbrella and started looking for a good spot to enjoy the sun. I, on the other hand, stepped out of the car slowly. I had to come up with a plan of action. ✱

"Maybe it won't be too hard to keep from swimming," I thought. "I could always hunt for seashells, play in the sand, or chase the birds. I could even buy ice cream to eat. By that time, it would probably be time to leave."

"Hurry up, Sonya!" Katie shouted, running toward the ocean. "Beat you into the water!"

The sand was hot, and it sank under my feet as I walked slowly after Katie. I couldn't help noticing some greenish-brown, rope-like things lying on the beach. I wondered what they were. They looked gross, so I made sure that I didn't step on any. They might sting. The water ahead looked uninviting.

Just as I reached the edge of the water, I froze. The ocean kept inching closer and closer, lapping at my feet.

"Why are you stopping?" Katie asked, standing in water up to her waist.

"I'm not coming in the water just yet," I said. "I have to put my beach towel down."

"Well, hurry up so we can surf the waves."

I headed back to where Uncle Jack and Aunt Lisa had set up the umbrella and spread out their beach towels. Our spot was right next to a lifeguard's chair.

"That's good," I thought. "If I get into any trouble, the lifeguard can save me."

Uncle Jack was reading his book, and Aunt Lisa was rubbing sunscreen onto her legs. "Good idea," I thought.

"May I use some of that?" I asked, sitting down on the towel beside her. I have never been sunburned. I tan easily, but this would give me something to do so I wouldn't have to go into the water just yet.

It wasn't long before Katie came running toward me. I hoped that maybe she was done playing in the water and that we could do something else for a while. She sat down beside me and watched as I slowly spread the sunscreen all over my skin.

"Let's build a sandcastle," I suggested.

"Not now—we can do that after we play in the water," Katie replied.

"How about finding some seashells to take home?"

"Sonya, are you afraid of the water?" Katie asked.

"No, of course not! Why would you think that?"

"Because ever since we decided to come to the beach, you've acted different. And now you're taking forever to get ready to go into the water!"

"Well, I'm not afraid of the water," I replied, standing up. I glanced up at the lifeguard, making sure she was still there, and headed off for the water.

"Aren't you coming?" I called to Katie as I marched right into the water. It was so cold that I had to grit my teeth. The water foamed up higher and higher around my ankles and legs.

Katie ran in behind me, grabbed my hand, and started walking out toward the bigger waves. I was getting more scared with each step. All these "what if" questions kept going through my mind. "What if I was knocked down by a wave? What if a jellyfish stung me? What if an octopus got me?"

The water rose above my knees to my thighs. Far ahead, I saw a giant wave gathering speed. I was sure that Katie would turn back, but she kept on walking. The wave thundered toward us. I dropped Katie's hand and turned around to go back, but the water was above my waist and I could hardly walk.

Just then, I felt something touch my foot! Whatever it was slid over my foot and wrapped itself around my ankle! "An octopus!" I screamed, as the giant wave crashed over my head and knocked me down. The next thing I knew, I was all the way under and fighting hard to stand up. I couldn't catch my breath! I finally got my head out of the water, but that thing still had a hold on my ankle and seemed to be pulling me under! "HELP! HELP!" I heard myself scream.

Suddenly, I felt strong arms around me, lifting me out of the water. I was gasping for air.

"Are you okay?" a voice asked. I looked up and saw the lifeguard's face. I was back on the beach, but my heart was still beating hard. Katie, Uncle Jack, and Aunt Lisa hurried over to see if I was injured.

"What happened? Are you okay?" Aunt Lisa asked, rubbing the sand off my face and arms.

"There was something—an octopus—around my ankle! It was pulling me under."

Katie looked at my ankle. Then she reached down and pulled off a piece of that strange, rope-like thing. "It's just seaweed," Katie said, wrapping the seaweed around her shoulders. "It's got me!" she screeched and fell onto the sand, giggling.

"That's enough, Katie," Uncle Jack said. "Come on, girls. I think some ice cream might taste pretty good right now."

Katie threw the seaweed away and ran ahead of her parents toward the ice-cream stand.

I just stood there feeling pretty silly. First, Katie guessed that I was afraid of the water, and now everyone thought I was afraid of seaweed! Maybe Katie regretted that she'd asked me to come visit.

I noticed the lifeguard was still standing nearby. I didn't want her to think I was a total loser, so I mumbled, "Thanks for saving me."

"You know, I used to be afraid of water, too, when I was your age," she said.

"You were?" I was too surprised to ask how she knew I was afraid.

The lifeguard smiled at me. "I was afraid to even put my head in the water! Then one day somebody dunked me. It really made me mad. So I decided it would be better to learn how to put my own head underwater than to have someone else do it for me."

She winked at me and started to walk back to her chair.

"Listen," she called over her shoulder, "come back after you eat your ice-cream cone, and I'll show you what I did."

I couldn't believe a lifeguard was ever afraid of the water! Maybe there was hope for me after all.

Then I saw Katie running toward me. "What kind of ice cream do you want, Sonya?"

"Chocolate and vanilla!" I shouted as I ran up to meet her.

Later that day, the lifeguard taught me how to put my head under the water, and Katie showed me how to surf the waves. I hope Uncle Jack has another day off tomorrow so we can come back to the beach.